Written by JD Green
Illustrated by Jennifer Naalchigar
Designed by Nicola Moore

First published by HOMETOWN WORLD in 2018
Hometown World Ltd
7 Northumberland Buildings
Bath
BA1 2JB

www.hometownworld.co.uk

Follow us @hometownworldbooks

ISBN 978-1-78553-829-2
Printed in Italy
HTW_PO201809

ISABELLE YOU'RE AMAZING!

Hometown World

Isabelle is **helpful**.

She gives this mix a beating.

SPLAT!

And when that cake's had time to bake,

she'll help out **with**

the

eating.

Isabelle is **caring**.

She's friend to birds and bees,

and **bugs**, and **slugs**, and dogs, and frogs,

and even **cats with fleas!**

Isabelle's a **rOck stAr!**
Each time she hears a song,
she sings aloud but does not care
if all the words are wrong!

Isabelle's so happy.

Her smile goes from ear-to-ear.

Just spending time around her

leaves you feeling full of cheer.

Isabelle is **sporting**.
You'll always see her **grinning**.

Not **everything** comes easily.

She practises **a lot!**

And that's how she's developed

the **AMAZING** skills she's got.

Isabelle's a **brave** girl.

This spider's **not** a threat!

She picks it up, **gives it a name**

and keeps it as **her pet!**

There's always **fun** and **laughter**

each place Isabelle goes.

She likes to dance around a lot

and strike a funky pose...

COOL!

Isabelle's so **generous** with all her awesome toys.

She shares them out when playing with the other **girls** and **boys**.

THE BEST!

Isabelle's **AMAZING**.

What sets this girl apart

is that she's **cool**, and **brave**, and **fun**,

and has a **GREAT**
BIG
HEART!